Over in the Forest

Come and Take a Peek

By Marianne Berkes

Illustrated by Jill Dubin

Dawn Publications

Over in the forest
Where the clean waters run
Lived a busy mother beaver
And her little *kit* **one**.

"Build," said the mother.
"I build," said the **one**.
So they helped build a lodge
Where the clean waters run.

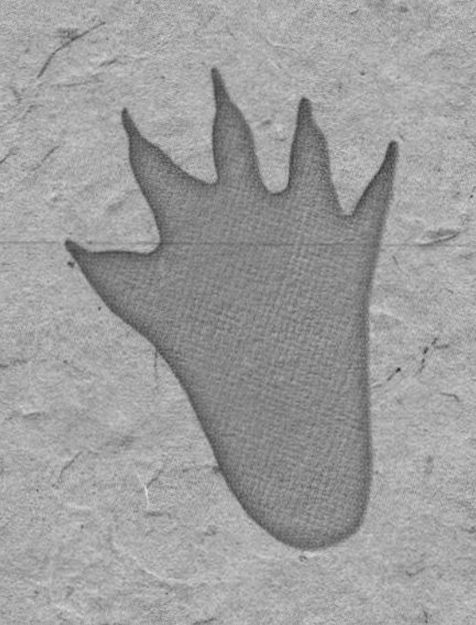

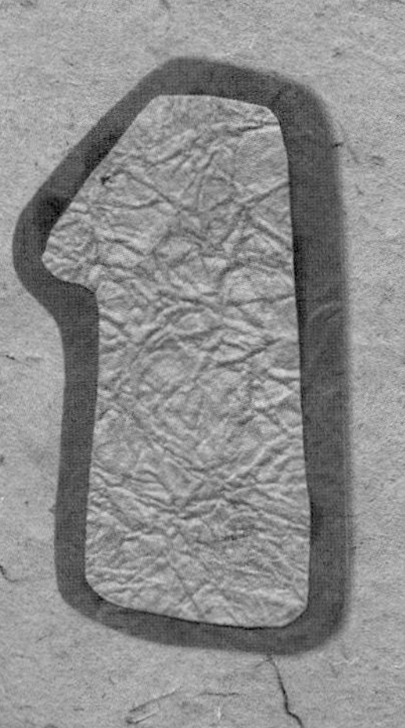

Over in the forest
In the early morning dew
Lived a hungry mother deer
And her little *fawns* **two**.

"Graze," said the mother.
"We graze," said the **two**.
So they grazed in the grass
In the early morning dew.

Over in the forest
In the hollow of a tree
Lived a shy mother 'possum
And her little *joeys* **three**.

"Ride," said the mother.
"We ride," said the **three**.
So they rode on her back
From the hollow of a tree.

3

Over in the forest
On the damp woodland floor
Lived a mother box turtle
And her little *hatchlings* **four**.

"Hide," said the mother.
"We hide," said the **four**.
So they hid in their shells
On the damp woodland floor.

4

Over in the forest
Where wild berries thrive
Lived an old mother turkey
And her little *poults* five.

"Scratch," said the mother.
"We scratch," said the five.
So they scratched on the ground
Where wild berries thrive.

Over in the forest
Doing acrobatic tricks
Lived a lively mother squirrel
And her little *kits* **six**.

"Leap," said the mother.
"We leap," said the **six**.
So they leaped through the trees
Doing acrobatic tricks.

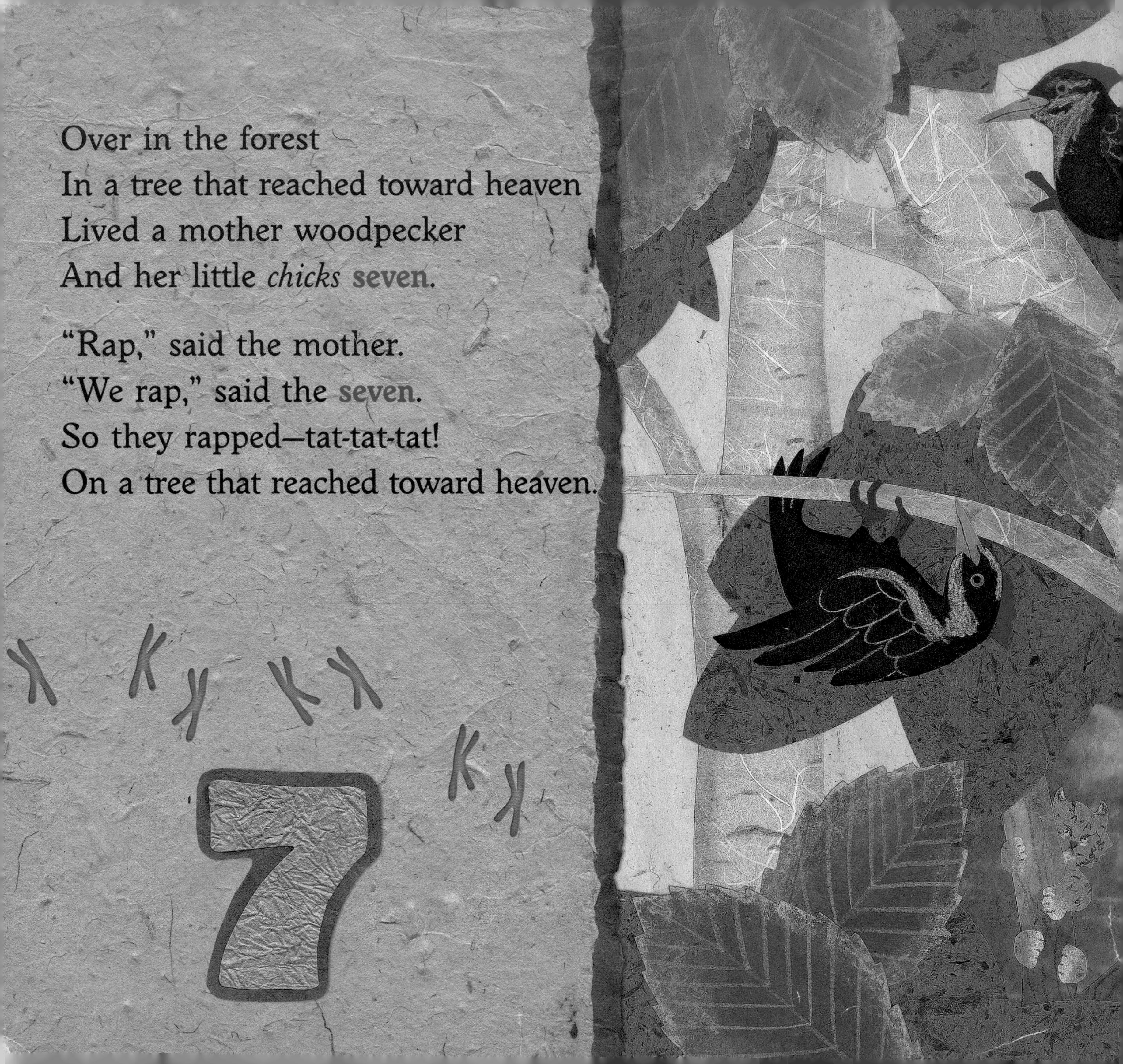

Over in the forest
In a tree that reached toward heaven
Lived a mother woodpecker
And her little *chicks* **seven**.

"Rap," said the mother.
"We rap," said the **seven**.
So they rapped—tat-tat-tat!
On a tree that reached toward heaven.

7

Over in the forest
Where they ate very late
Lived a mother raccoon
And her little *kits* **eight**.

"Dunk," said the mother.
"We dunk," said the **eight**.
So they dunked and they dabbled
As they ate very late.

8

Over in the forest
Near an evergreen pine
Lived a musky mother skunk
And her little *kits* **nine**.

"Spray," said the mother.
"We spray," said the **nine**.
So they sprayed stinky stuff
Near an evergreen pine.

Over in the forest
With his mate in a den
Lived a father red fox
And his little *kits* **ten**.

"Pounce," said the father.
"We pounce," said the **ten**.
So they pounced on the prey
That they brought to their den.

Over in the forest
Come on—let's take a peek!
While their parents all are resting,
The kids play "hide and seek."

"Find us," say the children,
"From ten to one."
Then go back and start over
'Cause this rhyme isn't done.

Over in the forest
There is so much to explore
Be sure to track the footprints
On the mossy woodland floor.

While you're counting footprints,
Also "spy" with your eyes
To find more forest creatures—
Every page has a surprise!

Fact or Fiction?

In this variation of the popular old song "Over in the Meadow," all the forest animals actually behave as they have been portrayed. Beavers *build*, squirrels *leap*, skunks *spray* and woodpeckers *rap*. That's a fact! But do they have the number of babies as in this rhyme? Not necessarily; that is fiction! Skunks rarely have nine babies, as in this story; they usually have four or five. While a mother deer will usually have one or two babies, a mother squirrel may have anywhere from three to fifteen, with five or six being common. A mother opossum and a mother red fox may have as many as twelve babies at one time. Woodpeckers typically lay four to seven eggs, and box turtles are likely to lay three to four eggs.

Nature has very different ways of ensuring the survival of different species in the forest. As indicated in this story, both father and mother fox take care of the babies until the kits can strike out on their own. Mother and father beaver also jointly take care of their kits, who usually stay with the parents for two years. Likewise, mother and father woodpecker watch over their nestlings until they are no longer helpless, but the mother skunk and mother squirrel raise their babies without help from the father.

What is a Forest?

Many people think of a forest as land covered with trees. That is true, but it is important not to overlook the wide variety of plants, as well as many animals, birds and insects that together make up the forest *ecosystem*.

The animals in this story live in a *temperate* forest with mostly *deciduous* trees. A *temperate* climate means there are warm summers and cold winters, but not extremely hot like the tropics or extremely cold like the polar regions. *Deciduous* refers to trees and plants that lose their leaves in the fall when there is less sunlight and the weather turns cold. Leaves turn brilliant colors and fall to the ground. The fallen leaves enrich the soil on the forest floor . In some forests that are primarily deciduous, evergreen trees, or *conifers*, also grow. Their needles are shed at various times but the trees stay green.

The "Hidden" Animals

GREEN TREE FROGS come in many different shades of green. They are especially active on damp or rainy evenings around the edges of ponds and lakes. The male makes a loud croaking sound, with the throat and sides of its body bulging out.

BLACK BEARS are the smallest and most common bear in North America. They are strong, agile, and quick. They can swim and climb trees. Black bears eat a wide variety of foods including nuts, berries, fruits, honey, insects, and small mammals.

BLUE JAYS are intelligent birds with a call that sounds like "jay! jay!" —one of a wide variety of sounds they make. They frequently chase other birds away from bird feeders. However, blue jays are primarily forest dwellers that particularly like acorns.

SALAMANDERS, like all amphibians, return to water to lay their eggs. When the eggs hatch, the larvae breathe with gills and swim, until they develop lungs for breathing air. Then they live under rocks in damp dark places.

COMMON RAT SNAKES prey on rodents, rabbits and birds. They are four to seven feet long. While not poisonous, when provoked they will stand their ground. Rat snakes are excellent climbers and often spend time in trees.

COYOTES are intelligent omnivores that have adapted to many different environments, feeding off human garbage and hunting mice and smaller mammals at night. They are good runners and swimmers.

BOBCATS are active day or night. They usually hunt small mammals, but can take on an animal as large as a deer. They use their claws and teeth to hunt on the ground, but are also good climbers and pounce on prey from trees.

The RED-TAILED HAWK hunts living things for its food. It soars and circles overhead dropping down on its prey in a steep dive, or stoop. This well-known bird nests in woodlands and feeds in open territory throughout most of North America.

OWLS silently swoop down on their prey with powerful talons. Their excellent hearing and vision help them hunt. After eating, an owl regurgitates pellets which contain bones, fur and feathers. Pellets are often collected by scientists who study an owl's eating habits.

PORCUPINES are nocturnal herbivores that can't see well. If attacked, a porcupine slaps its tail and shakes its hollow "rattle quills" toward the predator. The quills are sharp, come off easily, and can be painful to an attacking animal.

About the Animals

BEAVERS are large, sleek semi-aquatic rodents with flat tails and lustrous fur. They eat tree bark, leaves, roots and water plants. After gnawing on the bark of trees and tree limbs, they use the peeled sticks to build their dome-shaped homes (lodges.) These big-toothed builders carry timber between their teeth and mud with their front paws to create dams. The ponds around their lodges protect them from predators and provide access to food during the winter. Both parents care for one to four *kits* born in the spring. Kits usually stay with their parents for two years.

DEER graze, much like cows, eating a lot and digesting it later. A deer's stomach has four chambers. The first is where acids break down the tough plant fibers. The deer coughs up the food, re-chews it and passes it through the other three stomachs. A female deer, or *doe*, usually has one or two *fawns*. After birth, she licks them clean so predators can't smell their scent and keeps them in a sheltered spot called a "form." If there is more than one baby, the mother puts each one in a separate form so that if one is discovered by a predator, the other will be safe.

OPOSSUMS are the only marsupial in North America. Females give birth to *joeys* that climb into the mother's pouch where they remain for about ten weeks. After that they ride on their mother's back. Opossums eat insects, frogs, birds, snakes, small mammals, fruit and nuts. They are solitary and nocturnal, sleeping in a hollow tree or a ready-made abandoned burrow. Opossums have opposable thumbs on each hind foot to help them grip branches when they climb. When threatened or harmed, they "play possum," mimicking a dead animal, with the tongue hanging out and remaining absolutely still until the attacker loses interest.

BOX TURTLES can be found throughout the eastern, central and southwestern U.S. The box turtle in this story is the eastern box turtle, whose shell color and skin change with age. *Hatchlings* and younger turtles are often more vibrantly colored. Box turtles have a moveable hinge on the lower shell that allows them to hide completely in their shells, leaving no flesh exposed. They can be found under fallen logs or on moist ground under leaves. They are omnivores, feeding on a variety of animal and vegetable matter. They can live 80 years and are slow to mature.

WILD TURKEY females are smaller in size than males and have duller feathers. Males "gobble" with a mating call that can be heard a mile away. Females lay eggs on the ground in a depression lined with grass and leaves. They feed their *poults* after they hatch for a few days until the *poults* learn to fend for themselves. They *scratch* the ground for seeds and berries or climb small trees to feed on nuts, acorns and insects. Turkeys are cautious birds that fly or run at the first sign of danger. They live in open woodlands and perch on tree branches at night.

Tree squirrels have bushy tails, strong hind legs, powerful jaws, and strong claws for grasping and climbing. They are most active in late winter, when the mating season begins. A male leaps through the trees chasing a female at top speed. Female squirrels typically give birth to two to eight babies, sometimes called *kits,* in a nest called a *drey*. The tiny baby squirrel is virtually blind and dependent on its mother for the first six to eight weeks. Squirrels are predominantly herbivores that eat nuts and seeds, but some will eat insects, and small vertebrates.

Woodpeckers are mostly black and white with a splash of red on their heads. The male usually has an extra patch of color that a female does not have. There are many species of woodpeckers; the pileated woodpecker is portrayed in this story. They are easy to hear as they rap on trees with strong, pointed beaks. Their strong toes and sharp claws help them hold on to a tree trunk while their stiff tail feathers brace against the tree. They make small holes, looking for insects to eat. They also chisel roost holes in trees in which to raise their young *chicks*.

Raccoons are familiar nocturnal animals with masked faces and bushy ringed tails. Raccoon *kits* stay with their mothers up to nine months. These intelligent omnivores have an acute sense of touch. With the long, dexterous fingers on their front paws, they can even untie knots! Raccoons also use their paws to climb trees, and are very good swimmers. It is widely believed that raccoons dunk their food if they are near water. Some scientists say that this activity, called "dabbling," helps enhance their sense of touch. However, the definite answer is still known only to the raccoon.

Skunks are known for their smelly defense. Glands under their tails hold a musky liquid. If a skunk stamps its feet and raises its tail straight up with the back end pointing your way, watch out! The spray can travel up to 15 feet and the smell can carry a mile. A mother skunk nurses her *kits* in a safe den for about six weeks. Then she takes them out at night and teaches them how to hunt. They practice digging up worms, pouncing on mice and catching small fish. They will eat just about anything.

Red foxes have long bushy tails that they sweep around themselves to keep warm. Foxes have such sharp hearing that they can hear the underground movement of a mouse or gopher, and will pounce on it, often playing with it before eating. These omnivores are primarily nocturnal, but sometimes hunt by day. Together, male and female raise their *kits* for about a month after which the kits are able to strike out on their own. They are clever mammals that when hunted by wolves or man, will double back on their own tracks in order to confuse their enemies.

Tips from the Author

Outdoors: Be a Wildlife Detective

You can learn a lot about forest animals by simply looking and listening. With a grownup, sit *quietly* beside a trail to see what wildlife will come out of hiding.

LISTEN for sounds and try to find out who is making them—a woodpecker tapping, a bird chirping, squirrels chattering, an animal rustling leaves or digging.

LOOK for animal clues:

- Can you find tracks in the mud? What direction is the animal going? A great site to identify different animal tracks is: http://www.bear-tracker.com/mammals.html
- What has the animal eaten? Animal droppings, called "scat," can tell you what the animal has eaten, and what kind of animal it is.
- Be sure to look *up* into the trees for nests and other animal homes, and *down* on the ground for burrows and ant hills, or under rocks.
- Use a magnifying glass to get a closer look at leaves, moss and rocks. Look for tooth marks on twigs and branches, or scratches where an animal has climbed. Use binoculars to check out animals in the distance.

Indoors: Learning about the forest and its animals

Over in the Forest offers wonderful opportunities for extended activities. Here are some suggestions:

- Ten different verbs were used in the story to show how each animal behaves. Act them out as you read or sing the story. You may also want to add "actions" for the hidden animals.
- Ask: What were the ten parents called as babies? How many have the same "baby" name? What about the hidden animals? Do you know what they were called as babies?
- Introduce vocabulary that younger children might not be familiar with, e.g. *lodge, fawn, graze, poults, dew, musky, dunk and dabbled.*
- Discuss: Which of the twenty wildlife animals in this book live in your state?
- Create a forest diorama See: http://www.enchantedlearning.com/crafts/diorama/forest/
- Play "Who Am I?" Write two sentences describing an animal in this book, not mentioning which one it is, e.g. *I am the only marsupial in this story. I am shy.*
- Choose two forest animals in this book and compare them in a Venn diagram. http://www.graphic.org/venbas.html
- Write a diamante poem, comparing an animal in the story with the hidden animal on the same page. See www.readwritethink.org/files/resources/interactives/diamante/ to get started.
- Food is a basic need for all living things. Which forest animals are *omnivores*? Which ones are *carnivores*? Are there any *herbivores*?

Discover more in books . . .

Animal Tracks and Signs by Jinny Johnson (National Geo. Books, 2008)

Forest Animals (Animals in Their Habitats) by Francine Gaiko (Heinemann Library, 2002)

Forest Bright, Forest Night by Jennifer Ward (Dawn Publications, 2005)

A Forest Habitat by Bobbie Kalman (Crabtree Publishing, 2006)

Growing Up Wild: Exploring Nature with Young Children, (Council for Environmental Education, 2009)

Lost in the Woods by Carl R. Sams II (Photography, 2004)

Tracks, Scats and Signs by Leslie A. Dandy (Copper Square Pub., 1996)

The Tree in the Ancient Forest by Carol Reed-Jones (Dawn Pub., 1995)

Who Lives Here? Forest Animals by Deborah Hodge (Kids Can Press, 2009)

Wild Tracks by Jim Arnosky (Sterling, 2008)

The Woods Scientist by Stephen Swinburne and Susan Morse (Houghton Mifflin, 2002)

. . . and on the internet

http://www.kidwings.com/owlpellets/flash/v4/index.htm
http://www.enchantedlearning.com/biomes/tempdecid/tempdecid.shtml
http://www.nwf.org/wildlifewatch/
http://animals.nationalgeographic.com/animals/?source=NavAniHome
http://www.smokeybear.com/resources.asp
http://www.projectwild.org

Many more teaching and learning ideas from Marianne are available as free downloads at www.dawnpub.com. Go to "Teachers/Librarians," then "Downloadable Activities."

Tips from the Illustrator

Once the author's manuscript is complete, and the identity of each animal is decided, I use it to create the pictures. Since this book is about real animals in their environment, I have to make sure that what I create is accurate.

First I research as much as possible to learn how the animals actually look—both the adults and the babies. If I'm lucky I might see the real animal near where I live, like a squirrel, opossum, or deer. I look for pictures in books. And I do lots of searches on the computer. I keep a file on my computer of each animal. I print out some of the best examples and tape them to my bookshelf. This way I can refer to them as I draw each one. I always refer to several different sources, not just one. You can see some of the photos I used as research for this book.

These illustrations are collages—artwork that consists of many little things put together. First I draw a detailed pencil sketch for each page.

As I plan out each page, I keep in mind the color of the animals, the background, and how it will all fit together as a whole book.

I select paper for both color and texture to show the fur and feathers of the animals and the foliage of their environment. Compare the different papers I used as tree trunks for the woodpeckers and the squirrels. The woodpeckers are on birch trees that have white bark with a horizontal grain. The squirrels are on an oak tree with its brown bark with a vertical grain. It's fun to find just the right paper. I glue the animals together first, and then lay them out on the background, often trying differently textured and colored paper. The photo shows the mother skunk and all her babies as I plan their background.

When both the background and the animals seem right, I paste the animals on top of the background. I also may add details with colored pencils and pastels. This is the colored final art that gets printed in the book.

You'll get even more good ideas of how to do collage illustrations if you also read the tips I wrote in the books *Over in the Arctic* and *Over in Australia*. You can illustrate a forest, a garden, or even your own room! The possibilities are endless. Use your imagination, make it your own—and have fun.

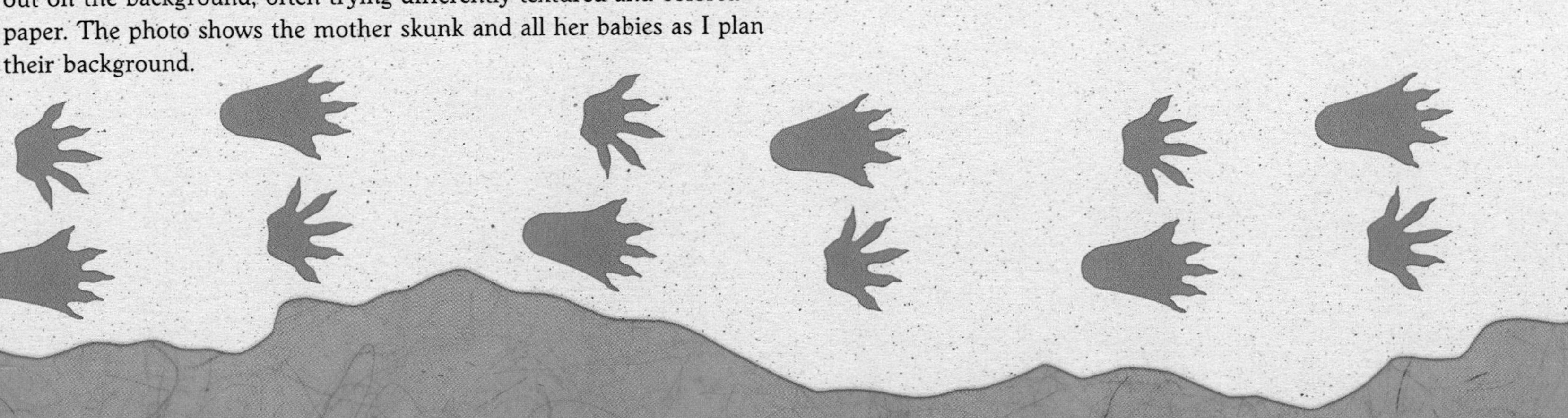

Over in the Forest

Sung to the tune "Over in the Meadow"

Traditional Tune
Words by Marianne Berkes

2. Over in the forest
In the early morning dew
Lived a hungry mother deer
And her little fawns two.

"Graze," said the mother.
"We graze," said the two.
So they grazed in the grass
In the early morning dew.

3. Over in the forest
In the hollow of a tree
Lived a shy mother 'possum
And her little joeys three.

"Ride," said the mother.
"We ride," said the three.
So they rode on her back
From the hollow of a tree.

4. Over in the forest
On the damp woodland floor
Lived a mother box turtle
And her little hatchlings four.

"Hide," said the mother.
"We hide," said the four.
So they hid in their shells
On the damp woodland floor.

5. Over in the forest
Where wild berries thrive
Lived an old mother turkey
And her little poults five.

"Scratch," said the mother.
"We scratch," said the five.
So they scratched on the ground
Where wild berries thrive.

6. Over in the forest
Doing acrobatic tricks
Lived a lively mother squirrel
And her little kits six.

"Leap," said the mother.
"We leap," said the six.
So they leaped through the trees
Doing acrobatic tricks

7. Over in the forest
In a tree that reached toward heaven
Lived a mother woodpecker
And her little chicks seven.

"Rap," said the mother.
"We rap," said the seven.
So they rapped—tat-tat-tat!
On a tree that reached toward heaven.

8. Over in the forest
Where they ate very late
Lived a mother raccoon
And her little kits eight.

"Dunk," said the mother.
"We dunk," said the eight.
So they dunked and they dabbled
As they ate very late.

9. Over in the forest
Near an evergreen pine
Lived a musky mother skunk
And her little kits nine.

"Spray," said the mother.
"We spray," said the nine.
So they sprayed stinky stuff
Near an evergreen pine.

10. Over in the forest
With his mate in a den
Lived a father red fox
And his little kits ten.

"Pounce," said the father.
"We pounce," said the ten.
So they pounced on the prey
That they brought to their den.

Marianne Berkes has spent much of her life as a teacher, children's theater director and children's librarian. She knows how much children enjoy "interactive" stories and is the author of many entertaining and educational picture books that make a child's learning relevant. Reading, music and theater have been a constant in Marianne's life. Her books are also inspired by her love of nature. She hopes to open kids' eyes to the magic found in our natural world. Marianne now writes full time. She also visits schools and presents at conferences. She is an energetic presenter who believes that "hands on" learning is fun. Her website is www.MarianneBerkes.com.

Jill Dubin's whimsical art has appeared in over 30 children's books. Her cut paper illustrations reflect her interest in combining color, pattern and texture. She grew up in Yonkers, New York, and graduated from Pratt Institute. She lives with her family in Atlanta, Georgia, including two dogs that do very little but with great enthusiasm. www.JillDubin.com

DEDICATIONS

For Scott, a wonderful father who loves exploring with his girls, Emily and Libby! Love — MB

To my mother with love — JD

Special thanks to June Parrilli and students at Hobe Sound Elementary school for the photo on the "Tips from the Author" page.

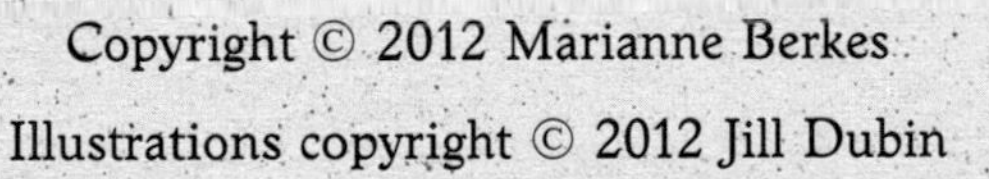

Book design and computer production by Patty Arnold, *Menagerie Design & Publishing*

Dawn Publications

12402 Bitney Springs Road
Nevada City, CA 95959
530-274-7775
nature@dawnpub.com

Library of Congress Cataloging-in-Publication Data
Berkes, Marianne Collins.
Over in the forest : come and take a peek / by Marianne Berkes ; illustrated by Jill Dubin.
p. cm.
Summary: A counting book in rhyme presents various forest animals and their offspring, from a mother beaver and her "little kit one" to a father red fox and his "little kits ten." Includes related facts and activities.
ISBN 978-1-58469-162-4 (hardback) -- ISBN 978-1-58469-163-1 (pbk.) [1. Stories in rhyme. 2. Forest animals--Fiction. 3. Animals--Infancy--Fiction. 4. Counting.] I. Dubin, Jill, ill. II. Title.
PZ8.3.B4557Ovf 2012
[E]--dc23

2011030879

Manufactured by Regent Publishing Services, Hong Kong
Printed January, 2012, in ShenZhen, Guangdong, China

10 9 8 7 6 5 4 3 2 1
First Edition

Also by Marianne Berkes

Over in the Ocean: In a Coral Reef – With unique and outstanding style, this book portrays a vivid community of marine creatures.

Over in the Jungle: A Rainforest Rhyme – As with *Ocean*, this book captures a rain forest teeming with remarkable animals.

Over in the Arctic: Where the Cold Winds Blow – Another charming counting rhyme introduces creatures of the tundra.

Over in Australia: Amazing Animals Down Under – Australian animals are often unique, many with pouches for the babies. Such fun!

Seashells by the Seashore – Kids discover, identify, and count twelve beautiful shells to give Grandma for her birthday.

Going Around the Sun: Some Planetary Fun – Earth is part of a fascinating "family" of planets. Here's a glimpse of the "neighborhood."

Going Home: The Mystery of Animal Migration – Many animals migrate "home," often over great distances. This winning combination of verse, factual language, and beautiful illustrations is a solid introduction.

Some Other Nature Awareness Books from Dawn Publications

Jo MacDonald Saw a Pond and *Jo MacDonald Had a Garden* are delightful nature-lover's (and gardener's) variations on "Old MacDonald Had a Farm." What a fun way to introduce kids to ponds and gardens. E–I–E–I–O!

Molly's Organic Farm is based on the true story of homeless cat that found herself in the wondrous world of an organic farm. Seen through Molly's eyes, the reader discovers the interplay of nature that grows wholesome food.

The "BLUES" Series – A comical team of cartoon bluebirds are crazy about REAL birds, and become quite the birdwatchers in *The BLUES Go Birding Across America*, *The BLUES Go Birding at Wild America's Shores*, and *The BLUES Go Extreme Birding*.

The "Mini-Habitat" Series – Beginning with the insects to be found under a rock (*Under One Rock: Bugs, Slugs and Other Ughs*) and moving on to other small habitats (around old logs, on flowers, cattails, cactuses, and in a tidepool), author Anthony Fredericks has a flair for introducing children to interesting "neighborhoods" of creatures. Field trips between covers!

Dawn Publications is dedicated to inspiring in children a deeper understanding and appreciation for all life on Earth. You can browse through our titles, download resources for teachers, and order at www.dawnpub.com, or call 800-545-7475.